Wolf Hill

In the Net

Roderick Hunt

Illustrated by Alex Brychta

Oxford University Press

Oxford University Press, Great Clarendon Street, Oxford, OX2 6DP

Oxford   New York
Athens   Auckland   Bangkok   Bogota   Buenos Aires   Calcutta
Cape Town   Chennai   Dar es Salaam   Delhi   Florence   Hong Kong
Istanbul   Karachi   Kuala Lumpur   Madrid   Melbourne   Mexico City
Mumbai   Nairobi   Paris   São Paulo   Singapore   Taipei   Tokyo
Toronto   Warsaw

and associated companies in
Berlin   Ibadan

Oxford is a trade mark of Oxford University Press

Printed in Hong Kong

2

Chapter 1

It was Gran's birthday. Loz and her Nan gave her a spade.

'Happy birthday!' said Loz. 'Guess what this is?' She gave Gran a spade-shaped parcel.

'Well,' laughed Gran. 'Is it a spade, I wonder? I need a new one.'

Nan told Gran to shut her eyes.

Loz went outside. She came back with another present. It was a wheel barrow. It had a big pink bow on the front.

'You can open your eyes, now,' said Loz.

Gran looked at the wheel barrow.

'Oh, thank you,' she said. 'It's just what I wanted.'

Gran loved gardening. She had a patch of ground near the canal.

'Now I've got a new spade you can help me, Loz,' said Gran. 'You can use the old one.'

Loz groaned, but she did help Gran. It was a good thing she did.

Chapter 2

Later, Loz and Gran went to the patch. Loz pushed the new wheel barrow. Gran took the new spade.

Suddenly Gran stopped in surprise. Three men were standing by her shed.

The men were looking at the patch next to Gran's. Nobody looked after it. It was full of weeds. Gran called it the Jungle.

One of the men was smoking a cigar. He was wearing a smart suit. He pointed at the Jungle.

'OK, you two,' he said. 'I want this garden dug.' He looked at Gran's patch. 'I want it looking like this one.'

'But, Boss . . . .' said one of them.

The man with the cigar turned to go. 'Get digging,' he said.

One of the men came over to Gran and Loz.

'Hey, Lady,' he said. 'Can we borrow your spade?'

Chapter 3

Loz went home at lunch time. Nan
wanted her home by one o'clock.

After lunch Loz called for Najma.

'What shall we do?' Najma asked.

'I don't know,' said Loz.

In the end they went to help Gran.
'She'll be down at her patch,' said
Loz.

Gran had finished digging. Loz and
Najma saw her talking to Mr
Morgan. Gran was pointing at the
two men in the next patch.

The men were hacking at the
weeds. They had Gran's old spade.

'They don't know much about gardening,' said Gran. 'They'll never dig it with my old spade.'

'They've got smart shoes on,' said Najma.

'You don't wear smart shoes to go gardening!' said Loz.

'They're up to something,' said Mr Morgan. 'And it's not gardening!'

Chapter 4

The next day, Gran went back to her patch. Her shed door was open.

'That's funny,' she thought. 'I always keep it locked.' She called Mr Morgan. 'Someone has broken into my shed,' she said.

'You can't trust anybody,' said Mr Morgan. 'What's missing?'

Gran looked in the shed.

'Nothing,' she said. 'Nothing at all. Wait a minute! Someone's been using my new spade!'

Mr Morgan looked at the patch next to Gran's. 'Well, blow me down!' he said.

The patch had been completely dug. There wasn't a weed to be seen.

'Those men must have worked all night,' he said.

14

Gran sniffed. 'My shed smells funny,' she said. 'What is it?'

Mr Morgan sniffed. 'I'd know that smell anywhere,' he said. 'It's cigar smoke.'

'Wait until those men come back,' said Gran. 'Using my new spade without asking. What a cheek!'

Chapter 5

The men didn't come back. The weeks went by. Weeds began to grow. The patch next to Gran's looked untidy again. 'It's back to a jungle,' said Gran.

Gran had bought a big plastic net. She was going to grow runner beans up it. She asked Loz and Nan to help her.

'I can't put it up by myself,' said Gran. 'It's too big.'

Nan went to the patch. Loz and
Najma went with her. They helped
Gran put up the net.

'This is hard work,' said Najma.

At last the net was up. It went right
across Gran's patch.

'This net is huge,' said Nan. 'How many runner beans do you need?'

Gran looked at the net. Nan was right. The net was too big.

They didn't know how important the net would be.

Chapter 6

'Come and have a cup of tea with me,' said Mr Morgan. 'It's my birthday today.'

'I didn't know,' said Gran.

'Birthdays don't mean much at my age,' he said. 'But I bought myself a cake – just for a treat.'

Mr Morgan had two old chairs in his shed. He set out a flask of tea and two cups.

'Come and sit down,' he said.

Gran and Mr Morgan sat down. Gran looked tired.

'You work too hard,' said Mr Morgan. 'You spend hours on your patch.'

'I enjoy it,' said Gran.

Gran felt sleepy. It was warm in the shed. Soon, she fell asleep.

'I'll leave her to sleep,' said Mr Morgan. 'I'll wake her up later.' He went back to work on his patch.

Mr Morgan forgot Gran was asleep in his shed. He locked the door and went home.

Chapter 7

Loz was fast asleep. She felt Nan shaking her.

'Laura! Wake up!' said Nan. She sounded worried.

Loz rubbed her eyes. 'What's the matter?' she said.

'It's Gran,' said Nan. 'Something's wrong.'

Loz sat up. 'What do you mean?'
she asked.

'I keep phoning,' said Nan. 'There's
no answer. We'll have to go to her
house.'

Loz got dressed quickly. She felt
worried, too. Gran was never out late.
What if she was ill?

Loz and Nan ran round to Gran's house. There were no lights on.

'Look,' said Nan. 'The curtains are still open. She hasn't come home.'

Loz felt sick. 'She must still be down in her patch. Perhaps she's ill.'

'We'll need help to get her home,' said Nan.

'Yes,' said Loz. 'Ask Najma's dad to help.'

Chapter 8

Najma lives next door to Loz and Nan. Nan knocked the door. She told Mr Patel about Gran.

'I'll get my car,' he said.

Najma woke up. She came
downstairs. Loz told her about
Gran.

'I want to come, too,' she said.

'Get dressed quickly, then,' said Mr
Patel.

They went to Gran's patch in Mr Patel's car. It was dark everywhere. Mr Patel had a torch. Gran was nowhere to be seen.

'That's funny,' said Nan. 'Her shed's still open. She hasn't put her new wheel barrow away. Her spade is still out. So is her rake.'

Najma squeezed Loz's hand. 'Try not to worry,' she said. 'I'm sure Gran's all right.'

'I hope so,' said Loz.

'Well,' said Mr Patel. 'Gran's not here. I think we should tell the police.'

Chapter 9

Gran woke up with a start. It was very dark. She couldn't think where she was. Her neck was stiff and her back hurt.

Gran sniffed. She could smell tar and onions.

'Oh dear,' thought Gran. 'I'm still in Mr Morgan's shed. I've been asleep.'

Gran tried the door, but it was locked. 'Oh no,' she said. 'I'm locked in.'

Then she heard a noise. She looked out of the dirty window.

Three men were digging in the jungle next to her patch. They were talking softly. They had a lamp which gave out a dim light.

'Those men are back. How
strange,' said Gran. 'They're digging
a hole.'

She saw them pull a bundle out of
the hole.

Gran did a silly thing. She banged
on the door and shouted.

'Help!' she called. 'I'm in here.'

Chapter 10

Two cars stopped outside Mr Morgan's house. One was a police car. 'What do they want?' he thought. 'It's late at night.'

A police woman knocked at the
door. She had Nan with her.

'Sorry to disturb you, Sir,' she said.
'We're looking for Mrs King. She's
missing.'

Mr Morgan thought for a second.
'Oh no!' he said. 'She fell asleep in
my shed. I meant to wake her up.
But I forgot. I must have locked
her in.'

'Will you come and unlock the
shed?' asked the police woman.

'Oh dear,' said Mr Morgan. 'I'll just
put my shoes on.'

Nan told Loz and Najma. 'We think we know where Gran is,' she said. 'She went to sleep in Mr Morgan's shed. It looks as if she's safe and sound.'

Nan was wrong. Gran wasn't safe and sound. She was in danger!

Chapter 11

The shed door crashed open. A torch shone in Gran's face. The light hurt her eyes. Two men grabbed her. They held her by the arms.

'Ouch!' said Gran. 'Let me go. You're hurting me.'

'What did you see?' growled
another man. He blew cigar smoke at
Gran.

'Nothing,' said Gran. 'I've been
asleep.'

The men pulled Gran across to
the Jungle. Gran was frightened.

'Stop it,' she said. 'I didn't see
anything.'

The dim light shone on the bundle.
It was a large bag wrapped in a
plastic sheet.

One of the men let go of Gran's arm.

'She's just an old lady,' he said. 'Tie her up. Then put her back in the shed.'

'You won't tie me up!' said Gran.

She pushed the other man as hard as she could. Then she ran for it.

Chapter 12

Suddenly a light shone across the patch.

'It's a police car,' shouted one of the men. He grabbed the bundle. 'Get out of here!'

The men began to run. They ran across Gran's patch. The man with the cigar ran into Gran's spade. 'Ouch!' he yelled.

Then he stepped on Gran's rake. The handle shot up. It made a thud as it smacked against his head.

The other two men ran into Gran's net. They both fell down. They tried to get up. The net wrapped itself round them. The men couldn't get away.

The policeman pulled out his handcuffs.

'Well, well, well!' said the police
woman. 'It's Fingers Foster and his
gang.'

The policeman looked in the
bundle. It was full of silver.

Chapter 13

Gran was pleased. The story was on the TV news. Her picture was in the newspaper. Nan read out the story.

Fingers Foster was a robber. He and his gang had stolen the silver months ago. They had hidden it in the patch next to Gran's.

'It was my runner bean net,' said Gran. 'That's what stopped them.'

'They tried to do a runner,' said Loz. 'But now they've *been* caught!'

Everyone laughed.